DANIEL'S DUCK

An I CAN READ Book ®

DANIEL'S DUCK

Clyde Robert Bulla

PICTURES BY

Joan Sandin

HarperCollins*Publishers*

To Henry Walter Garland III

I Can Read Book is a registered trademark of
HarperCollins Publishers.

DANIEL'S DUCK
Text copyright © 1979 by Clyde Robert Bulla
Illustrations copyright © 1979 by Joan Sandin

Library of Congress Cataloging-in-Publication Data
Bulla, Clyde Robert.
  Daniel's duck.

  (An I can read book)
  Summary: Daniel decides he hates the duck he
has carved until the best wood-carver in
Tennessee admires it.
  [1. Wood carving—Fiction]   I. Sandin, Joan.
II. Title.
PZ7.B912Dan 1979   [E]   77-25647
ISBN 0-06-020908-9
ISBN 0-06-020909-7 (lib. bdg.)

Jeff and Daniel were brothers.

They lived in a cabin

on a mountain in Tennessee.

Jeff had a good knife.

He could carve with it.

He could carve things out of wood.

He made a dish.

He made a cup and a spoon.

His mother and father were proud.

"Some day," they said,

"you may be as good

as Henry Pettigrew."

Henry Pettigrew lived in the valley.

They had never seen him,

but they had seen his work.

He was a wood-carver.

Some said he was

the best wood-carver in Tennessee.

Henry Pettigrew carved animals.

His birds looked as if they could fly.

His horses looked

as if they could run.

All his animals looked real.

Jeff and his brother Daniel

had seen some of them in town.

"I want to carve an animal,"

said Jeff.

"I want to carve a deer or a turkey

or a bear like Henry Pettigrew's.

But animals are hard to do."

"I want to carve an animal, too,"

said Daniel.

"You're not old enough," said Jeff.

"Yes, I am," said Daniel.

"I could carve one if I had

a good knife and some wood."

"It takes more than a good knife and some wood," said Jeff.

"What does it take?" asked Daniel.

"You have to know how," said Jeff.

"It's hard to carve an animal."

"I know how," said Daniel.

"Let's see if you do,"

said his father.

He gave Daniel a knife like Jeff's.

He gave him a block of wood.

13

It was winter.

The nights were long.

15

"This is a good time
to sit by the fire and carve,"
said Jeff.
"I'm going to make something
for the spring fair."

Every spring

there was a fair in the valley.

It was time for people to meet

after the long winter.

It was a time to show things

that they had made.

Sometimes

they sold what they had made.

Sometimes

they traded with one another.

Father knew how to make

Indian moccasins.

On winter nights he made moccasins
to take to the fair.

Mother cut pieces of cloth.

She sewed them together

to make a quilt.

"This will be a warm quilt
for somebody's bed," she said.
"I'll take it to the fair."

"I'm going to make a box
for the fair," said Jeff.
"I'm going to carve little moons
on the lid."
He said to his brother,
"You haven't done anything
with your block of wood.
What are you going to make?"
"I have to think," said Daniel.

Days went by.

Then he began to carve.

"What are you making?" asked Jeff.

"You'll see," said Daniel.

One night Jeff looked
at what Daniel was carving.
He saw a neck and a head.
He saw a wing.
"Now I see," he said.
"It's a bird."
"It's a duck," said Daniel.
"You're not doing it right,"
said Jeff.
"Its head is on backward."
"I want it that way," said Daniel.
"My duck is looking back."
"That's no way to do it," said Jeff.

26

Father said, "Let him do it his way."

Spring came.

It was time for the fair.

Mother had made her quilt.

Father had made three pairs

of moccasins.

Jeff's box was done.

"It took a long time," he said.

"My duck took a long time, too,"

said Daniel.

"Are you sure you want to take it

to the fair?" asked Jeff.

"Yes," said Daniel.

They went down the mountain
in a wagon.

Father drove the horses.

They drove into town.

There were people everywhere.

Everyone had come to the fair.

Father took the quilt
and the moccasins.
He took Jeff's box
and Daniel's duck.
He left them at the hall.
The hall was a long house
in the middle of town.
"This is where the show will be,"
said Father.
"People are getting it ready now."

34

They walked down the street.

They saw the river.

They talked with friends.

Father said, "The hall is open."

They went to the show.

There were pictures

that people had made.

There were quilts and rugs

and baskets.

There were dolls.

There were coonskin caps.

"Where are the wood carvings?"

asked Daniel.

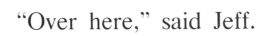

"Over here," said Jeff.

They went to the end of the hall.

The carvings were there on tables.

On a small table was a carved deer.

It was so beautiful

that people were quiet

when they looked at it.

Everyone knew it had been done

by Henry Pettigrew.

On a big table were the carvings
that others had done.

"I see my box," said Jeff.

"I see my duck," said Daniel.

Many people were looking

at the carvings.

They were laughing.

"What are they laughing at?"

asked Daniel.

Jeff didn't answer.

Someone said, "Look at the duck!"

Someone else said,

"That duck is so funny!"

More people came to look.

More people were laughing.

Now Daniel knew.

They were laughing at his duck.

He wanted to go away.

He wanted to hide.

Then he was angry.

He went to the table.

He picked up his duck

and ran with it.

He ran out of the hall.

Someone was running after him.

He ran faster.

He came to the river.

He started to throw the duck

as far as he could.

But he could not throw it.

A man had hold of his arm.

The man asked, "What are you

doing with that duck?"

"I'm going to throw it in the river!"

said Daniel.

"You can't do that," said the man.

"I can if I want to," said Daniel.

"It's mine."

"Did you make it?" asked the man.

"Yes," said Daniel.

"Why were you going to throw

it away?" asked the man.

"They all laughed at it," said Daniel.

"Listen to me," said the man.

"There are different ways of laughing.

The people *liked* your duck.

They laughed because they liked it."

"No. It's ugly," said Daniel.

"It *isn't* ugly. It's a good duck.

It made me feel happy.

That's why I laughed."

The man was not laughing now.

"You're hot and tired," he said.

"Come and rest in the shade."

They sat under a tree.

"Would you sell your duck?"

asked the man.

"Who would buy it?" asked Daniel.

"I might think of someone,"

said the man.

A boy and girl came up to them.

"How are you, Mr. Pettigrew?"

they asked.

"I'm fine," said the man.

The boy and girl went on.

Daniel said, "You're Henry Pettigrew!"

"Yes," said the man.

"I'm a wood-carver, too."

"I know that," said Daniel.

He was holding his duck.

He looked down at it.

It wasn't ugly.

It was a good duck.

Henry Pettigrew had said so,

and he knew.

"I saw your deer," said Daniel.

"I made it last winter," said the man.

"I've made lots of things.

My house is full of them."

Daniel said, "I wish—"

and then he stopped.

"What do you wish?" asked the man.

"I wish I could see

the things you've made," said Daniel.

"I'll show them to you,"

said the man.

"Maybe today, after the fair.

Shall we go back to the fair now?"

"Yes," said Daniel.

They got up.

The man was looking at the duck.

"Will you sell it to me?" he asked.

"No," said Daniel.

He held the duck a little longer.

Then he gave it to Henry Pettigrew.